P9-BXZ-797

Susan Laughs

JEANNE WILLIS

Illustrated by TONY ROSS

Henry Holt and Company • New York

Susan laughs,

Susan sings,

Susan flies,

Susan swings.

Susan's good, Susan's bad,

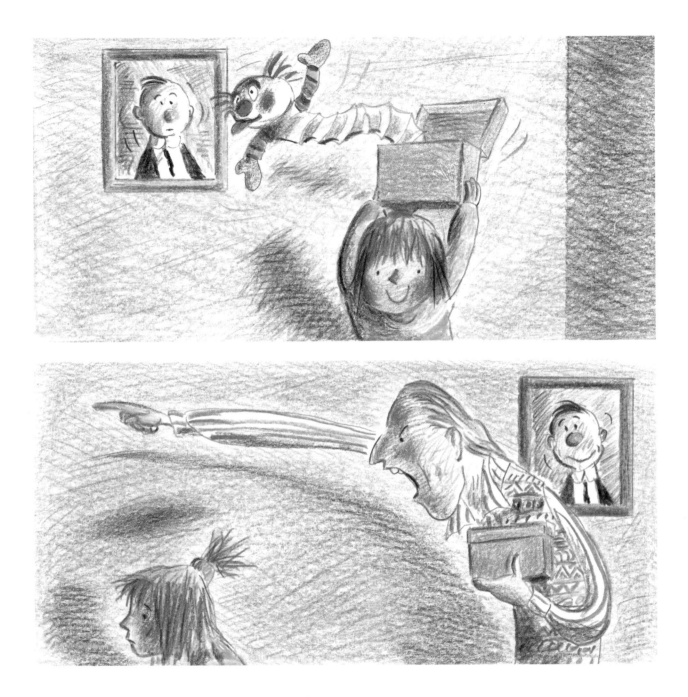

Susan's happy, Susan's sad.

Susan dances,

Susan rides,

Susan swims,

Susan hides.

Susan's shy,   Susan's loud,

Susan's angry,   Susan's proud.

Susan splashes,

Susan spins,

Susan waves,

Susan grins.

Susan's right,   Susan's wrong,

Susan's weak,   Susan's strong.

Susan trots,

Susan rows,

Susan paints,

Susan throws.

Susan feels, Susan fears,

Susan hugs, Susan hears.

That is Susan
through and through –
just like me, just like you.

Henry Holt and Company, LLC, *Publishers since 1866*
115 West 18th Street, New York, New York 10011

Henry Holt is a registered trademark of Henry Holt and Company, LLC

First published in the United States in 2000 by Henry Holt and Company, LLC
Published in Canada by Fitzhenry and Whiteside Ltd.,
195 Allstate Parkway, Markham, Ontario L3R 4T8.
Originally published in the United Kingdom in 1999 by Andersen Press Ltd.

Library of Congress Cataloging-in-Publication Data
Willis, Jeanne.
Susan laughs / Jeanne Willis; illustrated by Tony Ross.
Summary: Rhyming couplets describe a wide range of common emotions
and activities experienced by a little girl who uses a wheelchair.
[1. Emotions—Fiction. 2. Play—Fiction. 3. Physically handicapped—Fiction.
4. Stories in rhyme] I. Ross, Tony, ill. II. Title.
PZ8.3.W6799Su 2000 [E]—dc21 99-59560

ISBN 0-8050-6501-6 / First American Edition—2000
The artist used pencil and crayons to create the illustrations for this book.
Printed in Italy on acid-free paper. ∞
1 3 5 7 9 10 8 6 4 2